THOMAS RUTLING,

born a slave in Wilson County, Tennessee, in 1854.
He began to work on a farm at age eight. His
father was sold away before he was born.

MINNIE TATE,

born of free parents
in Nashville in 1857

ELLA SHEPPARD,

born a slave in Nashville
in 1851

ISAAC P. DICKERSON,

born a slave in
Wytheville, Virginia,
in 1850

MAGGIE PORTER,

born a slave in Lebanon, Tennessee, in 1853. One of the first pupils to attend
Fisk, she began teaching at the age of fifteen, but her schoolhouse
was burned down by those who were against schools for blacks.
She later returned to Fisk and joined the Jubilee Singers.

A BAND OF ANGELS

A Story Inspired by the Jubilee Singers

by DEBORAH HOPKINSON

illustrated by RAÚL COLÓN

❦ AN ANNE SCHWARTZ BOOK ❧

ATHENEUM BOOKS *for* YOUNG READERS

ACKNOWLEDGMENT

With deep thanks for her generous assistance to Beth Howse,
Reference Librarian, Special Collections, Fisk University,
who keeps Ella's spirit alive.
—D. H.

❖

With love to my sisters and nieces, Bonnie, Janice, Jamie, Kelly, and Haley;
and for Anne Schwartz, who knows about finding true songs.

—D. H.

For Talia and Justin

—R. C.

❖

Atheneum Books for Young Readers
An imprint of Simon & Schuster Children's Publishing Division
1230 Avenue of the Americas
New York, New York 10020

Book design by Michael Nelson

The text of this book is set in Cooper Light.
The illustrations are rendered in watercolor and colored pencil.

First Edition
Printed in Hong Kong
10 9 8 7 6 5 4 3 2 1

Library of Congress Cataloging-in-Publication Data
Hopkinson, Deborah.
A band of angels : a story inspired by the Jubilee Singers /
by Deborah Hopkinson ; illustrated by Raúl Colón.—1st ed.
p. cm.
"An Anne Schwartz book."
Summary: The daughter of a slave forms a gospel singing group and
goes on tour to raise money to save Fisk University.
ISBN 0-689-81062-8
1. Jubilee Singers—Juvenile fiction. [1. Jubilee Singers—Fiction. 2. Afro-Americans—Fiction.]
I. Colón, Raúl, ill. II. Title.
PZ7.H778125Br 1998
[Fic]—dc20
96-20011

My Aunt Beth calls herself a treasure-keeper. Her treasures are the stories about our family she keeps in her heart. Of all these treasures, my favorite is the story of my great-great-grandmother Ella.

⮵⮴

"Grandma Ella was born into slavery," Aunt Beth always begins. "But no one could chain her voice. Everyone said singing was part of that child the way swallows are part of the sky."

As Aunt Beth talks, I close my eyes and try to imagine a girl, long ago, who loved to sing. I see her slipping into an empty church to practice on the old piano there. She thinks she is alone, but everyone walking by outside stops to hear her songs.

"When Ella was fourteen the Civil War—and slavery—ended at last," Aunt Beth explains. "It was now the law that everyone, black or white, could get an education. But most schools and colleges were still only for white people. So when Ella heard about a new school for freed slaves in Nashville—Fisk School—she wanted with all her heart to go. But she had no money to pay for it.

"Ella began to keep a jar for coins, filling it with money she'd earn any way she could. At weddings, Ella played the piano. She scrubbed clothes for a few pennies. Yet when the time came for school to start, she'd saved only six dollars. She packed her things in a trunk anyway, and hired a wagon to take her to Nashville."

As Aunt Beth tells about the journey, I see Ella perched high on that wagon seat, eager for her first sight of Fisk School. When its shabby wooden buildings appear before her, she's not even disappointed. She's too excited to be going to school at last.

"The first person Ella met at school was Professor George White, the music teacher," Aunt Beth says. "She held out her money to him.

"'I'm afraid this is only enough for three weeks,' he told her.

"Ella must have felt discouraged standing before him with her little trunk, no bigger than a pie-box, at her feet. But she didn't let that stop her. She just kept working to make those three weeks longer and longer. She washed dishes and waited on tables in the dining hall. She gave music lessons to children in town. And late at night, when everyone else was asleep, she sat up with a basket of mending."

I imagine Ella, head bent over her work, needle flashing in the lamplight. A book is propped up on the table, so she can study while she sews. And I know my great-great-grandmother had a love of learning inside her that glowed like a warm, bright flame.

"No matter how tired Ella was, she was always ready for music," Aunt Beth lets me know. "The first time Professor White heard her singing, he invited her to join the school chorus. It wasn't long before she was playing the piano for the singers, too.

"Soon they had learned many classical pieces, and popular songs of the day that white people sang."

"But the chorus sang the old slave songs, too, didn't they?" I ask.

"Shhh, wait," Aunt Beth laughs. "We haven't got to that part yet.

"It was rainy that fall and the roofs leaked. The students' rooms were cold and damp. One night after practice Professor White had bad news for the singers.

"'Our buildings won't last much longer,' he said, 'and there's no money to fix them or build new ones. Unless something can be done, Fisk School will close.'

"All Ella's friends were working hard to pay for school. Jennie Jackson took in washing, Benjamin Holmes was a tailor, Greene Evans did odd jobs like painting and hauling gravel. If Fisk closed, they'd have no place to study. Their dreams for a brighter day would be lost.

"Sometimes songs arise from happiness, sometimes from sorrow. When Ella heard the news about her school, her heart was so heavy she just had to sing. She remembered a song she'd learned as a little girl, a song from slavery days.

"By then, few people were singing the old songs, and some were even being forgotten. They reminded people of their pain, of the hard days of slavery. But they were about hope, too. So Ella began to sing."

"Sing for me now, Aunt Beth," I whisper.

Aunt Beth holds me close and we sing together.

> *Swing low, sweet chariot,*
> > *Coming for to carry me home,*
> *Swing low, sweet chariot,*
> > *Coming for to carry me home,*
> *I looked over Jordan, and what did I see,*
> > *Coming for to carry me home?*
> *A band of angels coming after me,*
> > *Coming for to carry me home.*

Now comes the part of the story I like best. "What happened next?" I ask, though I already know. "Did the school close?"

"The school leaders were ready to give up. But not Professor White. He thought of a way he and the singers could help.

"'Our chorus is as good as any in the country,' he declared. 'And I believe people will buy tickets to hear us sing. If we give concerts up North, we can use the money to build a new school. Are you willing to try?'

"Ella spoke for all of them. 'Of course we will.'"

I think about how frightened Grandma Ella must have been before that long journey. She'd never ridden on a train, or been up North before. How she must have shivered in her thin coat and cloth shoes. But I also think Ella made herself be brave. The whole school was counting on them.

"As they traveled from town to town, those nine young singers faced many hardships," Aunt Beth tells me. "Often they were turned away from restaurants because their skin was black.

"One stormy evening no hotel would take them in. They trudged through the rain, until at last someone let them stay in a leaky shed. Ella slept wrapped in her coat, trying to keep warm.

"The chorus sang only the popular white songs they thought audiences wanted, like 'Annie Laurie' and 'Home Sweet Home.' Night after night Ella would put on her one fine dress, her face hopeful. But night after night she would look out to see just a few people in a dark, empty hall."

Aunt Beth's words make me feel like crying. And then I wonder if maybe Grandma Ella cried too, when no one was looking.

"Professor White didn't want to go back, but he didn't know what else to do. One evening before they went onstage, he spoke to the singers.

"'We did the best anyone could, but I'm afraid we must go home tomorrow,' he said. 'We haven't been able to raise even five hundred dollars—and our school needs five thousand.'

"The singers stood together without speaking. Then Ella turned slowly and walked across the lighted stage to take her place at the piano. The others filed in. Ella rested her fingers on the keys, wondering if this was the last time they'd ever sing together. Everyone in the hall was watching, waiting for her to begin.

"She took a deep breath. And somehow at that moment she found the courage to reach inside her heart—and bring forth her own song. In the silent hall her voice rang out clear and strong.

> *No more auction block for me,*
> *No more, no more;*
> *No more auction block for me,*
> *Many thousand gone.*

"How surprised Ella's friends were! This wasn't the popular melody they were supposed to sing. It was a song about the end of slavery, a song of freedom. And it was the first time they'd ever sung one of their own songs before an audience.

"The singers hesitated. But Ella's voice seemed to lift them up with her. And as their voices joined hers, like streams flowing into a deep river, they could feel everyone in the hall leaning forward to listen.

"When the song ended there was only silence. Afterward, some people said it had been like hearing a band of angels. Others found themselves in tears. All at once the hall erupted with shouts and cheers and applause.

"Professor White was smiling and clapping, too. 'Sing another of the old songs, Ella. They want to hear more!'"

Aunt Beth says that from that night on, Grandma Ella and her friends always sang the powerful songs of sorrow and courage they'd learned from their parents and grandparents. "They called them spirituals, or jubilee songs, because the word *jubilee* means a time of hope and freedom. And now that time had begun.

"The Jubilee Singers became such a success
they were invited to sing for thousands of people
all over the United States and Europe. They even
sang at the White House for President Grant and
in England for Queen Victoria."

Grandma Ella and the Jubilee Singers traveled
together for seven years, bringing back enough
money to make their small school into Fisk University.

Its most beautiful building is called Jubilee
Hall. Inside, in a place of honor, hangs a painting
of Grandma Ella and the singers. Whenever I
see her proud face there, I feel like singing,
too.

Today there are still Jubilee Singers, who keep
the old songs alive and share them with people
all over the world.

As her story ends, Aunt Beth is quiet, thinking about the past. I put my hand in hers. "When I grow up, I want to be a Jubilee Singer just like Grandma Ella."

Aunt Beth smiles. "Yes, but Grandma Ella would want you to do something else, too."

I know exactly what that is.

Grandma Ella worked so hard singing she never had the chance to finish her studies. None of those brave Jubilee Singers graduated from the school they loved so well.

But I will.

A Band of Angels is fiction, but it is based on real events and people. The character of Ella was inspired by Ella Sheppard Moore, who was born February 4, 1851, in Nashville, Tennessee. Her father was able to free himself and young Ella from slavery, but before he could buy freedom for Ella's mother she was sold away. Ella was raised in Cincinnati, where she took music lessons. At fifteen, she was left penniless when her father died. She arrived at Fisk School in 1868 with only six dollars.

Fisk was opened in 1866 as a school for former slaves and began offering college classes in 1871. That year, in a desperate attempt to save Fisk from closing, a music teacher named George White set out with a group of students on a singing tour to raise money. Although at first they only sang popular music of the day, they soon became famous for introducing spirituals to the world.

Ella Sheppard was the pianist for the Jubilee Singers on their historic concert tours, which raised enough money to save the school and build Jubilee Hall, the first permanent structure in the South for the education of black students. Ella later married George Moore, had three children, and located her mother and a sister. She died in 1914. Today her great-granddaughter is a librarian at Fisk University who shares the history of the Jubilee Singers with visitors.

Although none graduated from Fisk, the original Jubilee Singers were recognized with honorary degrees in 1978. Today, Jubilee Singers at Fisk University continue to keep alive a rich musical tradition that includes such songs as "Swing Low, Sweet Chariot," "Many Thousand Gone," and "Go Down, Moses."

Some Jubilee Songs

Swing Low, Sweet Chariot

Nobody Knows the Trouble I See, Lord!

Many Thousand Gone

The Gospel Train

This Old Time Religion

Go Down, Moses

Roll, Jordan, Roll

Steal Away

I'm So Glad

Room Enough

BENJAMIN M. HOLMES,

born a slave in Charleston, South Carolina, in 1846 or 1848. At about age seven he was apprenticed to a tailor and learned to read by studying signs on the streets as he made deliveries.

JENNIE JACKSON,

born free in Kingston, Tennessee

JUBILEE SINGERS 1871

GREENE EVANS,

born a slave in Fayette County, Tennessee, in 1848. During summer vacations from Fisk he taught in a log schoolhouse he helped to build.

ELIZA WALKER,

born a slave near Nashville in 1857